Hiya! My name Thudd. Best robot friend of Drewd. Thudd know lotsa stuff. What blood is made of. How body fight germs. What make heart beat. How brain work.

Drewd like to invent stuff. Thudd help! But Drewd make lotsa mistakes. Drewd invent shrinking machine. Now Drewd smaller than dust speck. Mosquito gonna shove Drewd inside Unkie Al! Thudd worried. Want to see what happen? Turn page, please!

Get lost with
Andrew, Judy, and Thudd
in all their exciting adventures!

ANDREW LOST

16

IN UNCLE AL

BY J. C. GREENBURG

ILLUSTRATED
BY JAN GERARDI

A STEPPING STONE BOOK™

Random House 🏠 New York

To Dan, Zack, and the real Andrew,
with a galaxy of love.
To the children who read these books: I wish
you wonderful questions. Questions are
telescopes into the universe!
—J.C.G.

To Cathy Goldsmith, with many thanks.
—J.G.

Text copyright © 2007 by J. C. Greenburg
Illustrations copyright © 2007 by Jan Gerardi

All rights reserved. Published in the United States by Random House
Children's Books, a division of Random House, Inc., New York.

RANDOM HOUSE and colophon are registered trademarks and A STEPPING
STONE BOOK and colophon are trademarks of Random House, Inc.
ANDREW LOST is a trademark of J. C. Greenburg.

www.randomhouse.com/kids/AndrewLost
www.AndrewLost.com

Educators and librarians, for a variety of teaching tools, visit us at
www.randomhouse.com/teachers

Library of Congress Cataloging-in-Publication Data
Greenburg, J. C. (Judith C.)
In Uncle Al / by J. C. Greenburg ; illustrated by Jan Gerardi. — 1st ed.
   p.   cm. — (Andrew Lost ; 16) "A Stepping Stone Book."
SUMMARY: When an electric fish shrinks Andrew, Judy, and Thudd
to the size of bacteria, they end up being injected by a mosquito
bite into Uncle Al's bloodstream, where they must battle germs,
parasites, and white blood cells.
ISBN 978-0-375-83565-0 (trade) — ISBN 978-0-375-93565-7 (lib. bdg.)
[1. Size—Fiction. 2. Blood—Fiction. 3. Cousins—Fiction.] I. Gerardi,
Jan, ill. II. Title.
PZ7.G82785Iu 2007   [Fic]—dc22   2006036838

Printed in the United States of America
10 9 8 7   First Edition

CONTENTS

ANDREW'S WORLD

Andrew Dubble

Andrew is ten years old, but he's been inventing things since he was four. His inventions usually get him in trouble, like the time he accidentally took the Time-A-Tron on a trip to the beginning of the universe.

Andrew's newest invention was supposed to save the world from getting buried in garbage. Instead, it squashed Andrew and his cousin Judy down to beetle size. They got hauled off to a dump, thrown up by a sea-gull, and carried off to the Australian rain forest on the back of a bird. Now, thanks to a mosquito, they're about to see what their uncle Al looks like—on the inside.

Judy Dubble

Judy is Andrew's thirteen-year-old cousin. She's been snuffled into a dog's nose, pooped out of a whale, and had her pajamas chewed by a Tyrannosaurus— all because of Andrew. Judy thought that nothing weirder could ever happen to her— until today.

Thudd

The **H**andy **U**ltra-**D**igital **D**etective. Thudd is a super-smart robot and Andrew's best friend. He has helped save Andrew and Judy from the exploding sun, the giant squid, and a monster asteroid. Now can he protect his microscopic buddies from the really weird stuff inside Uncle Al?

The Goa Constrictor

This giant fake snake is Andrew's newest invention. *Goa* is sort of short for **G**arbage **Go**es **A**way. The Goa is supposed to keep the world from getting buried in garbage by squashing rotting vegetables, green meat, and dirty diapers down to teensy-weensy specks. Unfortunately for Andrew and Judy, the Goa doesn't just shrink garbage. In two minutes and one stinky burp, the Goa can shrink anything—and anyone!

At first the Goa shrank Andrew and Judy to the size of beetles. But now, thanks to a shocking fish, the Dubble cousins are much, much smaller.

NYEEEEEEEEEE . . .

Andrew Dubble, smaller than a speck of dust, flopped onto his uncle Al's wrist.

Andrew, his pocket-sized robot friend Thudd, and his thirteen-year-old cousin Judy had just been plucked from an Australian river by their uncle Al. He had come looking for them with a rowboat and a powerful search-light.

Wowzers schnauzers! thought Andrew, bouncing on Uncle Al's skin. *We're too small to see! And it's nighttime, too.*

During their trip down the river, a shock from an electrical fish had shrunk them from the size of beetles to the size of bacteria.

When Uncle Al had opened their vehicle, the shiny, round Umbubble, they had tumbled out of it.

Ga-nuff . . . ga-nuff . . . ga-newww . . . Judy snored.

The shock that had made them small had also made Judy snooze.

With one hand, Andrew clutched the collar of Judy's jacket to keep her from falling off Uncle Al's wrist and into the river. With his other hand, he clung to one of Uncle Al's hairs.

Uncle Al shined his searchlight on the river.

Andrew looked up at Uncle Al. It was like looking up at the gigantic head of one of the presidents carved into Mount Rushmore.

Uncle Al's bushy eyebrows came together like two gigantic caterpillars. His frowning eyes scanned the dark ripples around his boat. "I wonder if they fell out when I opened the Umbubble," he said to himself.

"Uncle Al!" cried Andrew.

But Andrew's voice was much too small for Uncle Al to hear.

meep . . . "Purple-button time!" came a squeaky voice from Andrew's pocket. It was Thudd, Andrew's little silver robot and best friend.

In the middle of Thudd's chest were three rows of buttons with three buttons in each row. All of the buttons blinked green except for the big purple one in the middle. Pressing this button was the way Andrew, Judy, and Thudd could reach Uncle Al in an emergency.

Thudd pressed his purple button. It blinked three times and went off.

Nyeeeeeeeee . . .

The sound was close by. *What's that?* wondered Andrew.

Nyeeeeeeeee . . .

The sound kept getting louder.

NYEEEEEEEEEE . . .

The whining was so close and so loud that it hurt Andrew's tiny ears.

By the glare of the searchlight, Andrew made out something strange just above his head. It looked like a giant, hairy flower bud attached to a long, hairy stem. Andrew's eyes followed the stem up.

Way above, he glimpsed what was at the end of the stem—a horrible head!

"Yowzers!" he whispered. Two black eyes covered most of the head like a helmet. Long, hairy antennas stuck out from under the eyes.

Eek! "Mosquito!" squeaked Thudd.

Suddenly the hairy bud snapped open and slammed down over Andrew and Judy!

Eek! squeaked Thudd. "Mosquito snout! Called proboscis."

Inside the darkness of the mosquito snout, Andrew and Judy were squashed between two walls. Andrew couldn't move. He tried to push the walls.

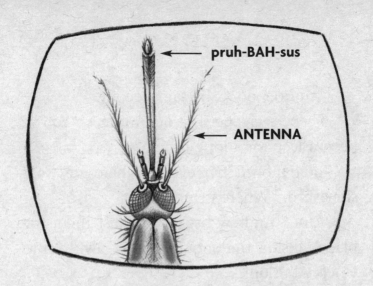

pruh-BAH-sus

ANTENNA

"Youch!" he said. The walls had razor-sharp edges, like blades.

The snout began to shove Andrew and Judy along Uncle Al's skin.

Eek! squeaked Thudd. "Mosquito look for good place to bite! Look for tiny blood tube called capillary. Near top of skin."

"What if Uncle Al swats the mosquito?" asked Andrew. "He'll crush us, too."

meep . . . "Mosquito light, light, light!" said Thudd. "Human not feel anything yet."

Ga-nufff . . . ga-nufff . . . ga-newww . . . snored Judy. She squirmed as though she were having a bad dream.

"Androoooo?" she said sleepily.

"Jeepers creepers!" said Andrew. "You've been asleep for a long time!"

Judy rubbed her eyes. "Where are we?" she asked. "Where's Uncle Al?"

"Um," Andrew began. But just then, the blades inside the snout started sawing into Uncle Al's skin!

Andrew sniffed a coppery smell. *Blood!* he thought.

Eek! "Mosquito snout gonna push Drewd and Oody inside Uncle Al!" squeaked Thudd. "Drewd got Schnozzle?"

Andrew shoved a hand into one of his pants pockets. He quickly pulled out two pairs of black goggles with noses attached and mustaches underneath. He handed one pair to Judy.

"Put on the Schnozzle, Judy!" said Andrew.

Judy pushed her face into Andrew's. "This isn't *Halloween*, Bug-Brain!" she yelled.

meep . . . "Quick! Quick! Quick!" said Thudd.

Andrew shoved the Schnozzle over his nose and hooked the earpieces behind his ears.

The blades of the mosquito's proboscis were sawing deeper and deeper into Uncle Al's skin. Andrew and Judy were on the very edge of the hole. One of the blades caught on Andrew's jacket and dragged him into the hole.

"Yowzers!" yelled Andrew.

"Aaaaaack!" hollered Judy, tumbling in after him.

A blasting spray drove them down and down. Without another scream, Andrew and Judy disappeared beneath Uncle Al's skin.

ATTACK OF THE BIG EATERS

Andrew tumbled over and over into warm, dark wetness. He reached for the mini-flashlight that he always kept on his belt loop.

The batteries are just about dead, he thought. *But I'll give it a try.*

He clicked the switch. The light went on—and it was bright!

Maybe the batteries got recharged when we got shocked by the electrical fish, he thought.

By the light, Andrew saw he was in a tight, twisty tube. He bounced against rubbery walls as a fast-flowing, chicken-soup-colored river dragged him along.

Uh-oh, thought Andrew. *We must be in a capillary.*

The rushing stream was stuffed with round red things that looked like doughnuts without holes.

The doughnut-y shapes were as big as Andrew. They felt like Jell-O when he was squeezed against them. Andrew and Judy got sandwiched between two of the squishy things.

These must be red blood cells! thought Andrew. *The guys that carry oxygen from our lungs.*

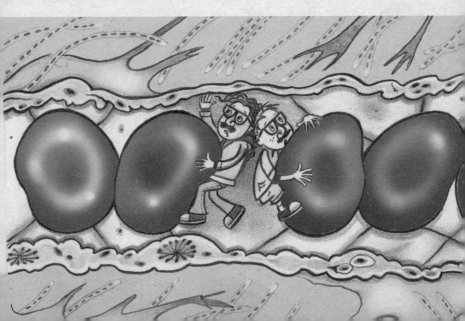

Andrew had been holding his breath as he bumped and tumbled through the tube. He felt he would burst if he didn't breathe now.

I designed the Schnozzle's mustache to get oxygen from water, he thought. *I sure hope it can get oxygen from blood, too.*

Andrew took a small breath through the Schnozzle nose. *Yay!* he thought. *The mustache picks up oxygen from blood. I can breathe!*

Now let's see if the thought-phones work.

From a pocket, Andrew pulled two tiny wire spirals and slipped them over Thudd's antennas.

Thudd! Judy! Can you hear me? thought Andrew.

"Yoop! Yoop! Yoop!" came Thudd's voice through the Schnozzle's earpieces.

"You've *really* done it this time, Bug-Brain!" came Judy's voice.

"Super-duper pooper-scooper!" Andrew said in his head. "You *can* hear me!"

All he had to do was think and the

Schnozzle's earpieces would send out his thoughts. And he could pick up the thoughts of others, too.

As Andrew tumbled through the river of blood, he turned up a tip of his shirt collar and unzipped a secret pocket. He pulled out what looked like a piece of rubber band with a black rubber cup at each end.

It was the Drastic Elastic, one of Uncle Al's inventions. It could keep anything connected to anything.

Andrew pressed one of the cups against the back of his neck. It stuck. He tossed the other cup to Judy, who was just behind him.

"Shove the Drastic Elastic cup against the back of your neck, Judy," he said. "It'll keep us from getting separated. No matter where we are, pulling on the Drastic Elastic will snap us back together."

Andrew tied Thudd to the Drastic Elastic, too.

"Oh, *great*!" said Judy. "If we ever get out

of Uncle Al, I'm going to invent something that will keep us *apart*!

"How on earth did you manage to get us into Uncle Al?"

meep . . . "Mosquito squirt us inside," said Thudd. "Mosquito got two tubes inside snout. One tube squirt spit into bite. Mosquito spit make animal not feel mosquito bite. Then other snout tube suck up blood. Female mosquito need blood for babies. Male mosquitoes not bite."

"This stuff we're in doesn't even look like blood," said Andrew. "It's yellow."

meep . . . "Yellow stuff called plasma," said Thudd. "Plasma kinda like river that carry red blood cells. Plasma carry food to body, too. Carry bad stuff away."

"How do we get it to carry us out of— Aaack!" Judy hollered. "Something just landed in my hair!"

Andrew felt something plop onto his head, too. Long, twisty spirals dangled over his eyes like wet pasta. A few of them sped off into Uncle Al's blood.

meep . . . "Bacteria!" squeaked Thudd. "Germs! Can make Unkie sick, sick, sick!"

Suddenly a giant white blob covered with shaggy tentacles squooshed through a slit in the capillary. The blob was bigger than the red blood cells. It squashed Andrew and Judy against the side of the rubbery capillary wall.

"Oh *NOOOOO!*" hollered Judy. "It's *horrible!*"

meep . . . "White blood cell," said Thudd. "Called macrophage. Macrophage mean 'big eater.' White blood cell eat up lotsa germs."

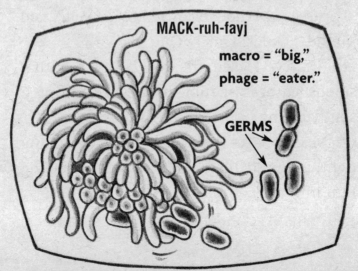

MACK-ruh-fayj

macro = "big,"
phage = "eater."

GERMS

The tentacles swarmed over Andrew in the tight capillary. They were touching his cheeks and tickling his neck. They were tugging off the spaghetti-like bacteria. Tentacles were poking into his nose!

Eek! squeaked Thudd. "Big-eater cell can tell that Drewd not belong inside Uncle Al! Big eater wanna eat Drewd!"

"Yaargh!" hollered Andrew, struggling to pull tentacles out of his nose.

meep . . . "Gotta hide!" said Thudd.

"Hide?" said Andrew. He battled the tentacles fiercely as the blood river swished them along. "There's nowhere to hide!"

meep . . . "Hide inside red blood cell," said Thudd. "Quick! Quick! Quick!"

Andrew kicked the red blood cell that smooshed against him. It was like hitting a soft balloon.

Macrophage tentacles were wrapping tightly around his chest. They were pulling him into the big cell!

Andrew shoved a hand into a pocket. Coins. Soggy packets of sugar. Two rough stones.

"Ooooog!" hollered Judy. "There are tentacles around my neck!"

Andrew reached back and pushed one of the stones toward Judy.

"Rip a hole in the red blood cell behind you," he said. "Hide inside."

Andrew slashed at the red blood cell in front of him. It was like cutting through a plastic bag. Red stuff oozed out through the slit.

Andrew struggled against the sticky tentacles of the big eater. They had him by the waist. They were dragging him into the big-eater cell. *How will I ever get inside the red blood cell before the big eater eats me?* thought Andrew.

3

IT'S JUST NOT RIGHT TO BE INSIDE YOUR UNCLE

Andrew slashed at the big-eater cell with his stone chip.

Woofers! thought Andrew. *This guy is a lot tougher than the red blood cell.*

Through the Schnozzle's earpieces, he could hear Judy's screams.

As Andrew sliced through the white blood cell, clear goo began to leak out of it.

The tentacles stopped wriggling and fell away. The white blood cell got floppy.

"Erk! Oook!" came Judy's voice.

Andrew felt her poking his back and kicking his legs.

"Judy, *relax,*" sighed Andrew, still catching his breath. "The big eater is dead."

"I know," said Judy. "I'm just trying to squash myself into this red blood cell."

Just then, Andrew caught sight of his own empty red blood cell getting dragged off by the rushing blood. He snagged the baggy cell with the toe of his shoe and squeezed inside.

"How did the big-eater cell know I didn't belong inside Uncle Al?" said Andrew.

meep . . . "All cells got special code on out-side," said Thudd. "Like label. Big eater read code. Code on Drewd cells say that Drewd not belong inside Unkie. Code on Unkie's red blood cell say it belong to Unkie.

"Big-eater cell is part of immune system. Immune system protect body from invaders."

WHAPPP!

The capillary shook.

"Got it!" came Uncle Al's voice.

"Uncle Al must have smacked the mosquito!" said Andrew.

"Why hasn't he answered our purple-button call?" asked Judy.

Another big-eater blob began squeezing through the capillary. Andrew and Judy pulled their heads inside the red blood cells. This time the big eater ignored them and wriggled off. More white blood cells followed like a herd of hairy ghosts.

"Where are those stupid things going?" asked Judy.

meep . . . "When body get hurt, when germs get in, body send signal to big-eater cells," said Thudd. "Lotsa big eaters come. Eat up bad stuff.

"Big eaters going to mosquito bite, maybe. Mosquitoes carry lotsa disease germs."

The red blood cell ahead of Andrew began to change color. It turned from bright red to dull red to dark red. Soon it was almost purple.

"It's getting harder to breathe," said Judy.

meep . . . "Cuz oxygen leaving red blood cells," said Thudd. "When red blood come from lungs, got lotsa oxygen. Color is bright red.

"As cell move through capillary, oxygen leave, go to other kindsa cells. Muscle cells. Brain cells.

"When oxygen leave, cell get dark. Cell gotta go back to lungs. Get oxygen. Turn red again."

The purple button in the middle of Thudd's chest began to blink.

"It's Uncle Al!" said Andrew.

The purple button popped open and a see-through hologram of Uncle Al zoomed out.

Uncle Al usually wore a crinkly grin. Not now. His eyes looked droopy and tired. "Andrew? Judy? Thudd?" he said softly.

When Uncle Al used his Hologram Helper to visit Andrew and Judy, he could hear them but not see them.

"Hi there!" said Andrew.

"We need help!" said Judy.

"Hiya, Unkie!" said Thudd.

"Where *are* you?" asked Uncle Al. "When I opened the Umbubble, you weren't inside."

"Um, we're actually inside *you*," said Andrew.

"SpongeBob SquarePants on a soda cracker!" exclaimed Uncle Al. His eyes were as round as golf balls. "How did *that* happen?"

"Well," said Andrew. "We started getting smaller after we got zapped by an electric fish."

"How small *are* you?" asked Uncle Al.

"We're as big as red blood cells," said Andrew.

"Good golly, Miss Molly!" said Uncle Al. "Red blood cells are *tiny*! Three thousand of them would make a one-inch-long parade!

"But how did you get inside me?"

"You know that mosquito you just smacked?" said Judy. "It shoved us into one of your capillaries."

"How are you guys able to breathe?" asked Uncle Al.

meep . . . "Drewd and Oody got Schnozzles to breathe with," said Thudd.

Uncle Al nodded. "And the Schnozzles and Hologram Helper are sending our thoughts back and forth.

"Now the big problem is getting you out of me."

4 GOING AROUND IN CIRCLES

Uncle Al rubbed his chin.

"Hmmmm . . . ," he murmured. "You guys are in my circulatory system."

"*Circulatory* system!" said Judy. "That means we're going around in *circles* inside you."

Uncle Al nodded. "Blood does go in circles. Very predictable.

"Do you have any idea where you are now?"

meep . . . "Blood is dark," said Thudd. "Going back to heart."

"Ah!" said Uncle Al. "You're in a capillary

26

headed to a vein now. Veins are the tubes that send blood to the lungs to get oxygen. Arteries are the tubes that send blood filled with oxygen to the body.

"Soon you'll get to my lungs," said Uncle Al. "Then you can crawl out of a capillary, into my lungs, and start climbing up.

"You'll get to my windpipe, the air tube that goes from my lungs to my nose. You climb up that and then, uh, crawl into my mouth."

"Eeeew!" Judy groaned. "That is *soooo* disgusting!"

Uncle Al chuckled. "Not more disgusting than getting flushed down the toilet, right? You've done *that* before.

"Uh-oh," said Uncle Al. "I'm having a power problem with the . . . I'll try to . . . and . . . back to . . .

"Hang . . . get to . . . heart. It . . . be . . . rough . . ."

Uncle Al disappeared, except for his lips. They were still moving. But Andrew and Judy couldn't hear a word. Then with a small pop, Uncle Al's lips disappeared.

The narrow capillary was opening into a wider passageway. Red blood cells no longer rushed along in single file. Now crowds of them were tumbling through the chicken-soupy plasma.

thumpa . . . thumpa . . . thumpa . . .

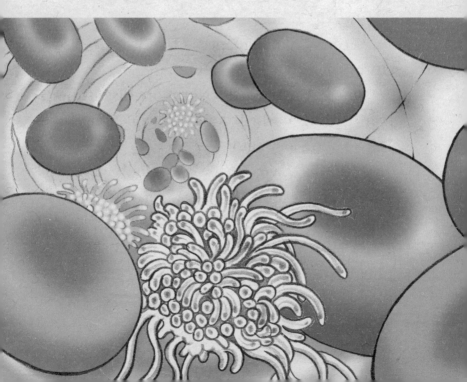

It was Uncle Al's heart beating.

White blood cells rushed like speeding jellyfish among the red cells.

A giant white blood cell whammed into Andrew's and Judy's red-blood-cell disguises and flung them apart.

"Androoooo!" hollered Judy.

Andrew tugged the Drastic Elastic sharply. The next instant, Judy's head banged against Andrew's.

"Youch!" hollered Judy.

"See?" said Andrew. "All I have to do is give the Drastic Elastic a big jerk."

"*You're* the big jerk, Bug-Brain!" said Judy, rubbing her head.

thumpa . . . thumpa . . . thumpa . . . thumpa . . . THUMPA . . .

Now Andrew didn't just hear the sound, he could feel it pounding like a drum.

"Uncle Al's heartbeat sounds really loud," said Andrew. "We must be getting close to his heart."

The blood river sped them along. Through the plasma and red blood cells, Andrew thought he saw giant pink tent flaps! They sprung open. Then they instantly slammed shut.

meep . . . "Flaps called heart valve," said Thudd. "Heart valve let blood into heart."

"What makes them open and close?" asked Andrew.

meep . . . "Electric signal," said Thudd. "Kinda like electric signal open garage door."

The next second, the heart flaps opened again. Andrew and Judy were sucked into a huge dark cave.

meep . . . "Inside heart now!" said Thudd.

Bzzzzzzzt . . .

A powerful tingle zipped from Andrew's head to his toes.

"Oofers!" he yelled. "I got an electric shock!"

meep . . . "Electricity come from Unkie Al's heart," said Thudd. "Part of heart called pacemaker. Pacemaker send electric signal to open heart valve. Send signal to make heart beat."

"We got shrunk by an electric shock," said Andrew. "If this shock makes us any smaller, we'll totally disappear!"

YOU'VE GOT TO HAVE GUTS

The blood river swooshed Andrew and Judy into a space crisscrossed by long, thick white strands.

"These things look like *tent* ropes," said Andrew.

meep . . . "Act kinda like tent ropes," said Thudd. "Called heartstrings. Tent ropes hold tent in place. Heartstrings hold heart flaps in place."

Andrew whammed against a tough, stretchy heartstring and bounced off.

The wide, fast river of blood zoomed Andrew and Judy up and up and around.

"It's like we're on a blood roller coaster," said Andrew.

"Aaack!" yelled Judy. "I'm gonna be sick!"

Whoosh . . . Whooosh . . . Whoosh . . .

"Sounds like a big storm," said Andrew.

meep . . . "Sound of Unkie Al breathing," said Thudd. "Leaving heart now. Going to lungs."

"Super-duper pooper-scooper!" said Andrew. "We can get out of Uncle Al soon!"

The blood carried them into a narrow passageway. They were in a lung capillary now.

Whoosh . . . Whooosh . . . Whoosh . . .

The blood cell ahead of Andrew was changing from deep purple to dark red.

"Woofers!" said Andrew. "It's getting easier to breathe!"

meep . . . "Red blood cells picking up oxygen from lungs," said Thudd, pointing to his face screen.

"So how do we get out of this stupid capillary?" asked Judy.

meep . . . "Get out same way big-eater cells get in," said Thudd. He pointed to faint lines in the capillary wall.

"Capillary wall made of single layer of cells. Kinda like patchwork quilt. Got spaces between cells where stuff get in, stuff get out. Food, oxygen, big-eater cells."

As the blood sped them along, Andrew ran his hands along the capillary wall, feeling for a space.

His fingers poked through an opening between two cells. He grabbed on to the edge of one of them. Judy slammed into him.

"Ergh!" Andrew groaned. The current of blood pulled at them. Andrew struggled to spread the cells apart.

Suddenly he felt something soft creep across his fingers, then across the top of his hand. Long, thin tentacles came slithering

through the slit in the capillary. A tentacle poked Andrew in the eye!

"Holy moly!" hollered Andrew. "A big eater!" He let go of the cell edges and pulled himself completely inside his red blood cell.

A stream of bright red cells whooshed Andrew and Judy off again.

meep . . . "Blood got lotsa oxygen now," said Thudd. "Gonna leave lungs."

Judy ran both hands along the capillary wall. "We'd better find another hole," she said. "Or else we'll be stuck in Uncle Al forever!"

The capillary tube widened.

meep . . . "Too late!" said Thudd. "Going back to heart now. Heart gonna pump blood into body."

The blood river drove them through the flaps of another heart valve. It slammed them into tough heartstrings. It whooshed them up again, then down.

"Holy moly!" said Andrew. "Where are we going now?"

meep . . . "Brain, maybe," said Thudd. "Foot, maybe. All kindsa places to go in Unkie Al."

Andrew and Judy tumbled through a cloud of prickly orange specks. The specks stuck to their red blood cells like dust.

Eek! squeaked Thudd. "Virus!"

"Viruses!" said Andrew. "Viruses give us colds and flus!"

meep . . . "And lotsa worse stuff, too," said Thudd.

"They're so tiny!" said Judy.

meep . . . "Virus tiny," agreed Thudd. "But virus can get into cell. Change way cell work. Can make Unkie sick, sick, sick!"

Suddenly long, sticky tentacles wrapped around Andrew's red blood cell, then Judy's.

"Oh no!" said Judy, ducking inside her cell. "These red blood cells were supposed to keep the stupid big eaters off of us."

"Wowzers schnauzers!" said Andrew, peeking out of his cell. "The big eaters are pulling the viruses off of our cells!"

They tossed about in the river of plasma as the big eaters crept over their cells, tugging at the prickly viruses.

After a while, Andrew felt no tentacles slithering outside his cell. He poked his head up. The big eaters were gone, and most of the orange specks were gone, too.

They were in a narrow capillary now. The blood sent them lurching through a zigzagging path.

meep . . . "In Unkie's intestines now," said Thudd. "Part where food get into blood through capillary spaces."

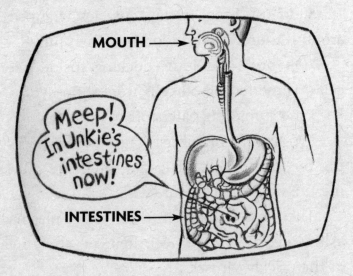

"If food gets in," said Judy, "we can get out. Let's find a space in this capillary."

Andrew and Judy ran their hands along the capillary wall, feeling for an opening.

"Found one!" said Andrew. He grabbed the edge of the cell and hung on as a stream of red blood cells rushed by him.

The opening was loose. Andrew quickly began pushing himself into it. He poked his head out of the capillary and into Uncle Al's intestines. "Holy moly!" he whispered.

6 WHO WANTS TO EAT A SCAB?

THUDD

Andrew was staring into a tube that looked bigger than a train tunnel. Sticking out from its walls were thousands of finger-shaped things that stretched and wriggled like strange worms.

Andrew pulled himself farther into Uncle Al's intestines. He pulled Thudd up, too.

"The blood is dragging me away!" came Judy's voice.

Andrew jerked the Drastic Elastic.

"Yoof!" cried Judy.

Andrew smiled. "She's back!"

He ran his hand over the finger-y things. They were as soft as velvet.

meep . . . "Called villi," said Thudd. "Stomach turn food into mush. Intestines break mush into tiny molecules.

"Villi pick up food molecules like sponge. Send molecules into blood to feed body."

A clump of rod shapes was slithering slowly toward Andrew.

"What's *that*?" asked Andrew.

meep . . . "Bacteria," said Thudd.

"What's going on up there?" shouted Judy from inside the capillary.

"Herds of germs are crawling around like slime carpets," said Andrew.

"Yuck-a-roony!" Judy exclaimed. "That's *soooooo disgusting*!"

"Noop! Noop! Noop!" said Thudd. "Lotsa good, good germs here.

"Animals not live without bacteria in intestines. Bacteria help break down food. Make vitamins."

"It's *still* disgusting!" said Judy from below.

Glurg glurg glurg . . .

A rumbling sound was coming from above.

Suddenly a waterfall of glop began pouring into Uncle Al's intestines.

meep . . . "Unkie's lunch coming!" said Thudd.

The villi wriggled and stretched wildly.

meep . . . "Villi trying to soak up lotsa food," said Thudd.

Andrew pulled himself back into the capillary before the flood of food hit him. He let the stream of blood carry them off.

"I'm glad we're not getting out of Uncle Al *that* way," said Judy.

The walls of their capillary widened. Streams of dish-shaped red blood cells and squid-like white blood cells swirled by. Small odd-shaped bits and pieces mixed among the crowds of cells.

"Where *are* we?" asked Judy.

meep . . . "Going down Unkie's leg now," said Thudd.

"Ouch!" came the voice of Uncle Al. It sounded far away. "Now, how did I get this sliver in my leg? Must have rubbed up against the side of the boat. There! I've got it."

Suddenly, ahead of Andrew and Judy, stringy strands began growing in the stream of blood. The strands tangled together like a messy spiderweb. Red blood cells and white blood cells were getting trapped in the web. A second later, Andrew and Judy were tangled in the web, too!

"Yaaargh!" yelled Andrew.

"Aaaaack!" hollered Judy.

Andrew ripped at the strands, but new strands kept appearing out of nowhere. He got more and more tangled.

meep . . . "Unkie got cut from sliver," said Thudd.

"When someone bleed, molecules in

blood come together, make sticky strings. Strings trap blood cells and other stuff. Make plug to stop bleeding. Called clot. Clot turn into scab."

"I'm not going to be part of anybody's *scab*!" said Judy, battling the strands. "How do we get out of here?"

meep . . . "Sticky strands made of same kinda stuff as spiderweb and meat," said Thudd. "Called protein. Remember how Drewd and Oody escape from spiderweb?"

"Yuck-a-rama!" said Judy, turning a little green. "We had to *eat* the spiderweb!"

"Yoop! Yoop! Yoop!" said Thudd. "Now gotta eat stringy stuff!"

"Uggggh!" said Judy, watching Andrew begin to gobble the sticky strands.

"Tastes like raw hamburger," said Andrew.

Judy rolled her eyes, but she pushed a small wad of the webby stuff into her mouth. "Tastes *awful*!" she gagged.

Andrew stuffed the strands into his mouth till he felt he would burst. Judy kept chomping away, too. When just a few strands were left, they ripped their way out.

Soon they were tumbling through Uncle Al's blood again.

meep . . . "In Unkie's foot now," said Thudd.

"Oof!" hollered Andrew, whamming into something soft that blocked their way.

"Umph!" yelled Judy, crashing into Andrew.

Andrew's flashlight lit up something awful.

"Yaaaaargh!" hollered Andrew.

"Nooooooo!" screamed Judy.

I'm face to face with the Loch Ness Monster! thought Andrew.

But the head of this monster had no eyes. It had no nose. It did have a huge, black mouth cave with four gigantic, jagged teeth at the top.

7 BLEEP, BLOOP, BLURP . . .

The horrible head waggled back and forth. Andrew and Judy desperately dodged away from the humongous mouth, but the rushing blood kept pushing them toward it. It was blocking the capillary.

meep . . . "Hookworm parasite!" said Thudd. "Parasite take food from other living thing, called host. This parasite wanna get food from Unkie Al.

"Hookworm chew through skin. Get under skin. Creep around. Suck blood. Lay eggs. Make lotsa little hookworms.

"Hookworm get into Unkie's foot when

Unkie walk through river. Lotsa parasites live in river water."

"Cheese Louise!" said Judy, fighting to stay away from the jagged teeth. "This monster's going to eat us, and poor Uncle Al will have disgusting worm families crawling around under his skin!"

"Don't worry," said Andrew, struggling to stay out of the horrid mouth. "The big-eater cells can tell the parasite doesn't belong inside Uncle Al. They'll be here any second."

meep . . . "Parasites got stuff that keep big eaters away," said Thudd.

"Hmmm . . . ," mused Andrew. "I have an idea."

He started spitting at the hookworm. "Come on, Judy! Help me! Spit!"

"What are you *doing*, Bug-Brain?" said Judy. "Trying to *insult* the hookworm to death?"

"I'm calling the big eaters," said Andrew. "Maybe they'll come if we mark the hookworm with some of *us*."

"*Aaaaaaack!*" hollered Judy. "There's a tentacle on my neck!"

Andrew turned to see a big eater squirming behind them. More tentacles were poking through the capillary walls.

Big-eater tentacles were everywhere! They swarmed over Andrew and Judy as they lashed out at the hookworm.

meep . . . "Drewd and Oody not wanna get between big eaters and dinner!" said Thudd. "Gotta get away!"

Andrew looked around. Another big eater was slithering through the capillary wall. As it pulled itself inside, Andrew held the slit open and wriggled out—and into another capillary. Judy was right behind him. The warm blood rushed them along again.

Judy rolled her eyes. "Well, *that* was pleasant," she said.

The red blood cells were turning darker.

"It's getting harder to breathe," said Andrew.

meep . . . "Blood going back to heart, back to lungs. Can try to get out through lungs again.

"Knock, knock. Who there? Boo. Boo who? Don't cry! Hee hee hee!"

"Thudd!" said Andrew. "What's going on? Why are you telling knock-knock jokes?"

Thudd's face screen went dark and the buttons on his chest stopped blinking.

"Oh no!" said Andrew. He pulled Thudd from his pocket and gave him a shake. "I think Thudd's thought chips are getting soggy. The last time this happened, he told elephant jokes. He was in bad shape.

"I painted him with three coats of Never-Wet, but it must be wearing off."

Andrew pressed Thudd's reset button. Thudd's gumdrop-shaped feet gave a little kick. The buttons on his chest began to blink green again, but not as brightly as before.

bleep . . . "Dewd? Oogy?"

"Are you okay, Thudd?" asked Andrew.

bloop . . . "Kinda," said Thudd woozily.

"Hang in there, buddy," said Andrew. "We'll get you dry soon."

blurp . . . "Thunkoo, Drewp," said Thudd.

Thumpa! Thumpa! Thumpa!

THUMPA! THUMPA!

They were getting near Uncle Al's heart again. It was beating faster than before. They were traveling at breakneck speed.

"Woofers!" said Andrew, somersaulting through the red blood cells. "The blood is moving so fast!"

gleep . . . "Unkie Al doing lotsa stuff, maybe," said Thudd. "Or Unkie Al scared, maybe.

"Heart beat fast when someone work hard. Heart beat fast when someone scared. Body need lotsa energy, lotsa oxygen. Heart rush blood to body."

THUMPA! THUMPA! THUMPA! THUMPA!

Andrew could see the heart valve ahead of them. It was opening. They were sucked into the right side of the heart and pumped out so quickly that the heartstrings were a blur.

The blood rushed them through the lungs too fast to find spaces in the capillary walls. Instantly, they were pumped to the left side of the heart. With a powerful squeeze, it zoomed them off into Uncle Al's body again.

Red blood cells smacked into Andrew like big rubber rafts. Andrew accidentally jerked the Drastic Elastic and Judy's head bonked into his.

Now it felt like the bloodstream was rushing them up and up.

Maybe we'll go to Uncle Al's nose, thought Andrew. *We could get out from there.*

Suddenly Andrew tingled all over. "Electricity!" he said.

meep . . . "Drewd and Oody in Unkie's brain now," said Thudd. "Brain use electric signals to send messages."

Andrew noticed that his arms and legs were poking out of his red-blood-cell disguise. *Uh-oh,* he thought. *I'm getting bigger!*

"Oofers!" cried Andrew. He was stuck in the capillary like a cork in a bottle.

8 A SHOCKING SITUATION

"Erf!" hollered Judy, slamming into Andrew. "What's going on?"

"I'm getting bigger," said Andrew. "That's why I'm stuck. And you're as big as I am. It's the electricity."

"What'll we do now?" asked Judy.

"We have to get out of the capillary," said Andrew.

He struggled to push apart a tight space between the cells.

"Wowzers schnauzers!" exclaimed Andrew. Through the opening, his flashlight beam showed white spidery shapes connected by long strands.

"So this is Uncle Al's brain! It looks like a weird web!"

meep . . . "Brain is web made of neuron cells," said Thudd. "Neuron is long, thin cell that connect to other neuron cells. Send electric messages to other parts of brain. To other parts of body.

"Gotta have neuron cells to walk. Talk. Move. Breathe. Think."

"Woofers!" groaned Andrew, squeezing himself through the capillary wall. His red blood cell was ripping.

He dragged himself out of the capillary and sat on top of it. He was awash in a warm, clear, watery soup.

Judy climbed out of the capillary and sat beside Andrew. Her red blood cell was tattered.

"Weird-a-mundo!" she said as she looked around.

"Youch!" said Andrew. "I keep getting zaps of electricity."

meep . . . "Unkie's brain cells sending messages," said Thudd.

Suddenly Thudd's purple button popped open and a beam of purple light zoomed out. At the end of the beam was Uncle Al. His bushy eyebrows came together in the middle of his forehead. He looked worried.

"Hey there, guys!" said Uncle Al. "I rowed the boat to shore. The Hologram Helper is working again, but I don't know for how long.

"Where are you guys, anyway?"

"We're inside your *brain,* Uncle Al!" said Judy.

"We had to get out of the capillary we were in," said Andrew, "because we were getting too big. I think the electricity from your heart and brain is making us grow."

Uncle Al smiled. "I'm glad you're getting bigger," he said. "But that means we'd better get you out of my brain soon."

Uncle Al rubbed his chin. "Let me see," he said. "The easiest way out of my brain is through my ear.

"Thudd, you know your way through the brain. Find the nerve that goes to my ear. It should be easy to get out from there."

gleep . . . "Knock, knock," Thudd began. "Who there? Pea. Pea who? Pea you! Drewd smell bad! Hoo hoo!"

Uncle Al shook his head. "Knock-knock jokes," he said grimly. "Thudd's thought chips are dangerously soggy."

"I'm pressing his reset button," said Andrew.

pleep . . . "Blokey-dokey, Bunkie Al," said Thudd. "Can get Shmewd and Doody to ear."

"Thudd," said Uncle Al. "I know it's hard for you to focus, but you've got to try. We're all depending on you."

Thudd pointed ahead.

meep . . . "That way," he said.

Andrew and Judy scrambled among the long, spidery arms of the brain cells like monkeys swinging through the jungle on vines.

"Your brain is *greasy,* Uncle Al," said Judy.

Uncle Al laughed. "That's because the nerves are covered with a layer of special fat," he said. "Kind of like the way electric wires are covered with rubber or plastic. Keeps the electrical signals going in the right direction."

Andrew and Judy kept getting little shocks from the nerves all around them. Andrew caught a glimpse of Uncle Al's hologram. His eyes looked as big as moons and his nose wrinkled up.

"What's wrong, Uncle Al?" asked Andrew.

"I just got a whiff of something awful," said Uncle Al. "Smells like a mix of stinky feet, dead fish, dog poop, and the baddest bad breath in the universe."

9 EGGBEATERS, AARDVARKS, AND ABRAHAM LINCOLN

THUDD

Uncle Al's eyes lit up. "You must be in the part of my brain that gets smell messages!" he said.

"When you smell something, your nose sends a signal to the part of your brain that deals with smell messages.

"You're messing around in the smelling part of my brain. My brain thinks it's getting signals from my nose."

"Sorry about the smell, Uncle Al," said Andrew, climbing through the nerve cells.

Uncle Al rubbed his eyes. "I'm seeing stars!" he said.

"You're stomping around at the back of

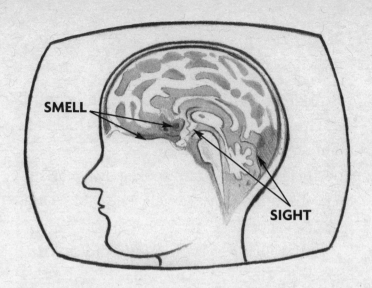

my brain. The part that gets signals from my eyes.

"But this means that you're going in the wrong direction. Thudd, are you okay?"

zleep . . . "Knock, knock . . . ," said Thudd.

Andrew pressed Thudd's reset button before he could say another word.

"Oops! Oops! Oops!" said Thudd. "Thudd make boo-boo. But Thudd know right way." He pointed left.

"I hope you're right," said Andrew. "Because I can feel myself growing. We'll wreck Uncle Al's brain if we get much bigger."

Andrew and Judy took a left and continued creeping through the tangle of Uncle Al's brain.

Uncle Al's hologram looked away. "Hammer, pliers, monkey wrench," he said. "Drill, scissors, eggbeater . . ."

Judy rolled her eyes. "You're not making any sense, Uncle Al," she said.

Uncle Al smiled. "That's because you're trekking through the part of my brain that stores the names of tools," he said.

"Strange-a-mundo!" said Judy.

They trekked on, slipping and sliding along Uncle Al's nerve cells.

"Crocodile, aardvark, rhinoceros beetle, giant squid," said Uncle Al. "Tyrannosaurus, bald eagle, humu humu nuku nuku apu ah ah fish."

"Cheese Louise!" said Judy. "We must have crawled into the part of your brain that stores the names of animals!"

"Right!" said Uncle Al.

Andrew and Judy pushed on.

"Abraham Lincoln, Chief Sitting Bull, J. K. Rowling, Queen Elizabeth, King Tut, Judy Dubble," chanted Uncle Al.

"The part of the brain for *people's* names!" said Andrew.

Uncle Al smiled. "That means you're going in the right direction," he said. "Good work, Thudd."

"Thunkoo," said Thudd.

"Ha ha ha!" Uncle Al laughed. "Hoo hoo!"

"What's so funny?" asked Judy.

"I feel like I'm being tickled," said Uncle Al. "Hee hee hee! But you're on track. Keep going! Hoo hoo!"

"Bluck!" blurted Uncle Al. His face scrunched up like a wad of paper.

"What's happening, Uncle Al?" asked Andrew.

"My mouth tastes like an old boot," said Uncle Al. "You're in the taste area of my brain. Ah! You must have moved. Now I'm tasting pepperoni pizza! Wish you could stay *there* for a while."

Thudd pointed up. Andrew and Judy pulled themselves higher.

Uncle Al chuckled. "Now I'm hearing, um, a rude sound and a toilet flushing," he said.

"Thudd, you're doing great work! You're in the part of my brain that gets sound messages from my ears."

"Thunkoo, Unkie!" said Thudd.

"Now you need to find the big nerve that leads to my ear."

Thudd looked around till he found a thick tangle of brain cells.

meep . . . "Big nerve!" he said. "This way!"

As they crept along, Andrew's backbone began to feel stretchy. "I'm growing again," he said.

"Me too," said Judy.

meep . . . "Thudd too!" squeaked Thudd.

As Andrew groped his way through the thick, soft clutter of brain cells, he found himself in a space that seemed to be filled with red pudding. He banged his head into something hard.

"What's this?" said Andrew. "Everything else inside Uncle Al is *squishy*!"

meep . . . "Nerve going through skull bone now," said Thudd.

"This can't be *bone*," said Judy. "It's full of *holes*! Bone is solid and *hard*!"

Uncle Al shook his head. "Parts of bones are solid and hard," he said. "But some bones, like skulls, have hard bone on the outside and spongy bone with lots of holes on the inside. Kind of like a bone sandwich.

"The red stuff inside the spongy bone is what makes red blood cells. It's called marrow.

"Thudd, find the little hole in my skull that takes you right into my middle ear."

"Yoop! Yoop! Yoop!" said Thudd. He pointed ahead and they crept on.

"Good golly, Miss Molly!" exclaimed Uncle Al. He was holding his head. "I feel dizzy. What are you guys up to?"

"Nothing," said Andrew.

"My foot got tangled in a nerve," said Judy.

"Ah!" said Uncle Al. "Must be a nerve that sends signals about balance from my ear to my brain."

"Inside my skull are three tiny loops. Inside these loops are super-tiny stones.

"When my head moves, the stones move. They send messages to my brain about my balance. But if you mess with my balance nerve, my brain gets the message that I'm dizzy."

"Sorry, Uncle Al," said Judy, scrambling ahead.

They came to a place where there was no marrow. The spaces in the spongy bone were filled with air.

meep . . . "Drewd and Oody can take off Schnozzles," said Thudd. "Can breathe air now!"

"Super-duper pooper-scooper!" shouted Andrew, pulling off his Schnozzle. He folded it flat and put it in his pocket.

"Now can we take off these stupid blood-cell disguises?" asked Judy. "Mine is a wreck, anyway."

"Yoop, yoop, yoop!" said Thudd. "No big eaters here."

Thudd pointed to a large dark hole. *meep* . . . "Drewd and Oody go through hole. Drop into middle ear."

Andrew went first.

"Erf!" he said, landing on his behind.

He gazed out into the shadowy space lit by his flashlight. "Looks like a bizarre-o cave!" he said.

"Ooof!" Judy dropped down on top of Andrew.

"What do we do next, Uncle Al?" asked Andrew.

"Where are you?" asked Uncle Al.

Andrew looked around. "There are three weird bony things at the top of this place," said Andrew. "One of them is touching a round white thing that looks like a trampoline on its side."

Uncle Al nodded. "The round white thing is my eardrum. The tiny bones help send sound messages from my eardrum to my brain," said Uncle Al.

The three bones became a blur as they vibrated at the sound of Uncle Al's voice.

"How big are you now?" asked Uncle Al.

"We're as big as one of those bones," said Andrew. "But we're growing every minute."

Uncle Al's eyebrows flew up. "Benjamin Franklin on a buttered bagel!" he exclaimed. "From the size of a microscopic red blood cell to the size of a grain of rice in minutes! This changes everything!"

AN EAR-LY LANDING

Uncle Al rubbed his chin.

"I had thought you could slip through the cells in my eardrum. The eardrum is just a thin piece of skin. But you're much too big for that now."

Andrew looked around the ear cave. His light fell on a round opening near his feet. He leaned down to look into the hole, but all he could see was a dark tunnel.

"There's a hole under the ear bones," said Andrew. "It's big enough for us to squeeze into."

meep . . . "Eustachian tube," said Thudd. "Connect ear to back of nose."

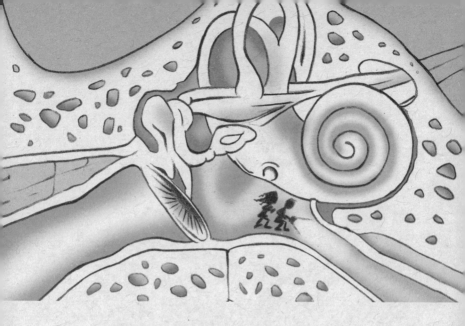

Uncle Al smiled. "You guys can slip into the Eustachian tube and get to the back of my nose," he said. "From there, you can crawl down through my nose and out!"

"Eeeew!" said Judy.

"Okey-dokey, Unkie," said Thudd.

"Let's go!" said Andrew.

He slipped into the Eustachian tube and Judy followed. The way down was steep and tight and damp. As Andrew slid down, the tube got tighter and tighter. He had to push himself through.

I'm growing fast, he thought.

Andrew plopped onto a gooey, slippery shelf in a dark cave much larger than the inside of Uncle Al's ear.

meep . . . "Drewd at back of Unkie's nose now," said Thudd. "Lotsa nose goo here, called mucus."

Andrew felt something moving him backward. Below him, under the goo, he could make out a carpet of tiny, waving hairs. They were working like a slimy conveyor belt, dragging him to the back of Uncle Al's nose.

"What's moving me?" asked Andrew.

meep . . . "Little hairs under mucus called cilia," said Thudd. "Mucus catch dirt. Catch germs. Cilia move mucus from back of nose to back of throat. Then mucus get swallowed."

"Whoa!" Judy came sliding down and landed on a shelf-like place below Andrew. "I'm *soaked* in Uncle Al's nose goo!" said Judy.

A strong wind whipped by them, dragging them backward through the goo. And in a second, the wind changed direction and nearly yanked them down from their slimy shelves.

"It's Uncle Al breathing," said Andrew.

Uncle Al's eyes squeezed shut and his mouth opened. "Uh-oh," he said. "You're ticklink the back of my nose. Ahm tryink not to shneeze."

Eek! squeaked Thudd. "Sneeze can go two hundred miles an hour. Fast as winds of hurricane! Fast as winds of tornado!"

Uncle Al's face was getting redder. His eyes were bulging. His cheeks puffed out like a chipmunk storing nuts for the winter.

"*AHH . . . AHHH . . . AHHHH . . .*"—Uncle Al looked as though he was about to explode—"*CHOOOOOOOOOO!*"

Suddenly Andrew and Judy were flying through space like Superman and Super-woman.

"Yeoooow!" hollered Andrew. His stomach flip-flopped as he zoomed through the air. Everything was a blur.

He whammed into something soft and bounced away. He waved his arms to grab whatever he could. He caught something and hung on.

Andrew was hanging down into empty space and seeing double. He was dizzy from the flying and falling and flip-flopping. But he had a grip on something soft and tan.

Where am I? he wondered.

"Booooof!" hollered Judy from someplace above Andrew.

Andrew's eyes began to focus. "I'm on Uncle Al's ear!" he cheered.

Suddenly it seemed that five large tree trunks were zooming toward them.

"Fingers!" yelled Andrew.

"Uncle Al's fingers!"

The fingers gently scooped them up.

Before they knew it, they were in Uncle Al's palm looking up at his smiling brown eyes.

"Welcome back, guys!" said Uncle Al. "There's a kitchen next door, and I'm going to make you the tiniest pepperoni pizza anyone has ever had!"

TO BE CONTINUED IN ANDREW, JUDY, AND THUDD'S
NEXT EXCITING ADVENTURE:

ANDREW LOST

IN THE DESERT!

In stores January 2008

TRUE STUFF

Thudd wanted to tell you more about big-eater cells and bones, but he was busy keeping Andrew and Judy from being munched by a parasite and lost in Uncle Al's brain. Here's what he wanted to say:

• There are many things outside of our bodies—bacteria, viruses, poisons, and tiny animals—that could hurt us if they got inside. We have immune systems made up of cells and molecules that patrol our bodies like armies to destroy dangerous things.

• All the cells in our bodies are marked with special molecules. This molecule code tells our immune system that these cells are part of us and should not be attacked.

Blood cells have markers that say they belong to a group called a blood type. Your blood cells have markers for one of these blood types. If you got into a bad accident and needed blood, you would have to get it from someone with your blood type. If you received a different type of blood, your immune system would attack and destroy the strange cells. The attack would not only destroy the new blood cells, it could kill you, too.

• Macrophages have such big appetites, they actually eat until they die! After you scrape your knee or get a cut, do you ever see gooey yellow or white stuff around it? This is called pus. Pus is actually made up of dead white blood cells!

• Blood cells are red for the same reason that rusty iron is red. Iron turns red when it combines with the oxygen in the air. Blood cells have iron. Iron is what carries oxygen from our lungs to our bodies. When the iron in blood combines with oxygen, blood looks red.

• If you look at your wrists, you will probably see veins where your blood looks blue. Inside your veins, this blood is really deep red or purple. But it looks blue because you're seeing it through your skin.

• Are you allergic to cats or pollen or bee stings? Poison ivy or peanuts? None of these things are dangerous all by themselves. Many people are not bothered by them at all.

An allergy means that your immune system is confused about its enemies. It mistakes harmless stuff for dangerous stuff—and attacks. The problem is that the weapons of the immune system can cause lots of damage to your body, too—resulting in sneezing, itching, swelling, fevers, and worse.

• When your body is attacked by bacteria or viruses, the temperature of your body may get hotter. You have a fever.

Fevers are one of the ways your body fights infections. For example, higher temperatures help to kill some bacteria. When you have a fever, your body hides some of the food that bacteria need to survive. Your immune system also makes more of the cells needed to attack the invaders.

So making a fever is one of the ways your immune system helps you to get well. Fevers aren't dangerous unless they get too high.

Aspirin and aspirin-like medicines are often used to lower fevers. But if you're under nineteen years old, you should never take aspirin or aspirin-like medicines to lower a fever unless a doctor tells you to. Aspirin-like medicines could cause you to develop Reye's syndrome, a problem worse than a fever or a cold.

• Our immune system can turn against our own cells and attack them. When this happens, we actually become allergic to ourselves. Such attacks by our immune system can lead to diseases like asthma and intestinal problems.

Most people think that parasites, such as hookworms, are disgusting and unhealthy. However, scientists have discovered that people who have hookworms aren't attacked by their own immune systems. These parasites make stuff that controls the immune system and keeps it from attacking.

For some serious diseases, doctors are actually giving people parasites to eat!

• When you get a cold or the flu, it takes a while for your immune system to make the special army needed to defeat the "bad guys." That's why it takes about ten days for you to get better. However, once your immune-system army has met and defeated the bad guys, it will be instantly ready to wipe them out if the two forces meet again—before you get sick.

That's how vaccines (vack-SEENZ) work. For example, a shot of flu vaccine prepares your body to recognize and destroy the enemy as soon as they meet. And you don't get sick!

• It's easy to think of bones as solid and rocky and not really alive. But bones are changing all the time.

If bones didn't change, you couldn't grow taller and bigger. And your bones couldn't heal if they broke. As you get older, the shape of your face will change as the bones in your skull change.

Bones change because they're made up of two kinds of cells that have opposite jobs. Osteoclasts [AHS-tee-uh-klasts] are constantly breaking down old bone. Osteoblasts [AHS-tee-uh-blasts] are always busy making new bone, mainly from the calcium in your milk and other food.

WHERE TO FIND MORE TRUE STUFF

Would you like to find out more about the weird and wonderful stuff that goes on in your body? Here are some books for you:

• *Body Warriors: The Immune System* by Lisa Trumbauer (Chicago: Heinemann-Raintree, 2007). When bad stuff attacks, your body goes into amazing action. See what happens!

• *The Magic School Bus Inside Ralphie: A Book About Germs* by Joanna Cole (New York: Scholastic, 1995). It gets pretty crazy inside Ralphie when germs invade.

• *Uncover the Human Body* by Luann Colombo (San Diego: Silver Dolphin Press, 2003). Want to see what you look like on the *inside*? You'll have fun putting yourself together—and taking yourself apart.

• *The Brain: Our Nervous System* by Seymour Simon (New York: Collins, 2006). Learn all about your squishy brain. And with all the great pictures, you'll feel like you're crawling into it!

Turn the page
for a sneak peek at
Andrew, Judy, and Thudd's
next exciting adventure—

ANDREW LOST
IN THE DESERT

Available January 2008

Excerpt copyright © 2008 by J. C. Greenburg.
Published by Random House Children's Books, a division of
Random House, Inc., New York.

HOT! HOT! HOT!

"Erf!" said ant-sized Andrew Dubble. He was inside an empty bottle cap, bouncing into his cousin Judy.

Their uncle Al had glued the bottle cap to the dashboard of his jeep. It made a safe perch for Andrew and Judy to see the Australian desert as Uncle Al drove through it.

"Get off of me, Bug-Brain," said Judy, shoving Andrew away. "It's *soooo* hot in here!"

"It's a rough trip through the desert, guys," said Uncle Al. "The air conditioner isn't working, so you'd better settle in for a long, hot, bumpy ride."

meep . . . "Desert air hot, hot, hot!" came a squeaky voice from Andrew's shirt pocket. "Desert sand even hotter. Can fry egg on desert sand."

It was Andrew's little silver robot friend, Thudd. Uncle Al had invented him.

The afternoon sun burned through the windshield. The yellow sand stretched on forever. Here and there, patches of tall, prickly grass looked like resting herds of spiny porcupines. Now and then, a scraggly tree poked up like a skeleton.

"The desert is like an empty planet," said Andrew.

Uncle Al shook his head. "It looks that way now," he said. "But lots of strange creatures are sleeping or hiding underground during the hottest hours. They'll come out to hunt when the sun goes down."

Oinga! Oinga! Oinga! came a sound from the front of the jeep. The jeep was slowing down.

Plunk . . . plunk . . . erk . . .

The jeep rolled to a stop. A ribbon of steam curled out from under the hood.

Uncle Al shook his head. "I'll find out what's wrong," he said. "And while I'm doing that, I want you guys to stay put. The desert is a dangerous place. Some of the most dangerous animals in the world live here. And not all of them sleep during the day."

"Okey-dokey, Unkie!" squeaked Thudd.

Uncle Al got out of the jeep and opened the hood. A cloud of steam puffed out.

"We've got a leak," yelled Uncle Al from the front of the car. "I need to check underneath the jeep. This may take a while."

The heat was making Andrew sleepy. He rested his head against the edge of the bottle cap.

Out of the corner of his eye, Andrew caught a glimpse of something moving. He turned to see a dark cloud whirling near the ground. It was spinning like a top and whipping up the sand. It was heading straight toward the jeep!

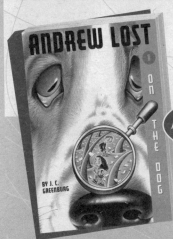

Bring magic into your life with these enchanting books!

Magic Tree House® series
by Mary Pope Osborne

The Magic Elements Quartet
by Mallory Loehr
Water Wishes
Earth Magic
Wind Spell
Fire Dreams

Dragons
by Lucille Recht Penner

Fox Eyes
by Mordicai Gerstein

King Arthur's Courage
by Stephanie Spinner

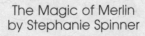

The Magic of Merlin
by Stephanie Spinner

Unicorns
by Lucille Recht Penner